Leo the Lion

Library of Congress Cataloging-in-Publication Data
Wagener, Gerda.
   [Leo Löwe. English]
   Leo the lion / by Gerda Wagener ; illustrations by Reinhard Michl;
translated from the German by Nina Ignatowicz.
      p.   cm.
   Translation of: Leo Löwe.
   Summary: An allegory about Leo the Lion who searches for someone
who will show him love and affection.
   ISBN 0-06-021656-5. — ISBN 0-06-021657-3 (lib. bdg.)
   [1. Lions—Fiction.   2. Loneliness—Fiction.   3. Allegories.]
I. Michl, Reinhard, ill.   II. Title.
PZ7.W123Le   1991   90-46272
[E]—dc20   CIP
                                                          AC

Leo the Lion

by Gerda Wagener

illustrations by Reinhard Michl

translated from the German by Nina Ignatowicz

HarperCollins*Publishers*

Leo was a lion.

Leo was a lonely lion.

Leo was the loneliest lion in the world.

Every evening he would stand outside Mr. Brown's house, press his nose against the windowpane and watch Mr. Brown stroke his pet cat, Katrinka.

Katrinka would stretch contentedly, then slowly climb up on Mr. Brown's lap and purr. That made Mr. Brown smile.

Sometimes when the wind whistled through the trees, Leo shivered from the cold; and when it rained, Leo got wet. And sometimes, when he got cold and wet, Leo sneezed.

"There's someone at the door, Katrinka," Mr. Brown would say, and he would get up from his easy chair to investigate. But Leo would always run and hide behind the big tree.

"Strange," Mr. Brown would say. "I thought I heard someone sneeze."

"Meow," Katrinka would reply. She let herself be stroked and purred contentedly as they went back inside.

Then once again Leo would go back and press his nose against the windowpane and wish that it were he, and not Katrinka, inside the warm house.

And every night when Mr. Brown put out the lights, Leo would walk home alone and sad.

One night Leo dreamed about Mr. Brown. Katrinka did not appear in his dream, only Mr. Brown and Leo. Leo sat on Mr. Brown's lap while Mr. Brown gently stroked his mane. Leo purred with pleasure. And even though Leo's purrs were louder than Katrinka's and the windowpanes rattled a little from his purring, Mr. Brown didn't mind. He kept stroking Leo's mane and smiling.

Leo stretched out with pleasure and fell off Mr. Brown's lap....

Leo sat up, startled.
It had been only a dream!

The next evening he was back in front of Mr. Brown's house. There was no wind and no rain. Even so, Leo sneezed.

This time when Mr. Brown opened the door to investigate, Leo did not hide behind the big tree.

"I thought I heard a noise," said Mr. Brown. "I thought I heard someone sneeze."

"I sneezed," said Leo. "I want to be petted like Katrinka."

Mr. Brown turned pale with fright and ran back inside the house and bolted the door. Katrinka jumped up on top of the cabinet and glared out at Leo.

Mr. Brown went to the window, but he didn't open it.

"You must understand," said Mr. Brown apologetically through the closed window, "you are much too big for me to pet."

But Leo didn't understand.

"I am big only on the outside," he told Mr. Brown. "Inside I am small and huggable."

"A lion will always be a lion," said Mr. Brown.

"Meow," agreed Katrinka.

Leo walked away, more dejected than ever.

When Leo woke up the next morning, the sun was shining. Leo didn't feel as sad and lonely. In fact he was almost happy as he strode into town determined to find someone who would not be afraid to pet him.

Leo walked into an ice-cream parlor.

"I want to ask you something," he said to the pretty waitress. "Would you please give me a tiny hug?"

"Aaaaaaah!" screamed the waitress, and she jumped up on the counter.

Everyone else in the ice-cream parlor rushed out the door. They were all afraid of him.

Leo sadly licked strawberry ice cream off the floor and left without giving the waitress another glance.

A short while later Leo climbed over the fence at the public swimming pool. Since it was a hot day, there were a lot of people around the pool. Some lay in the sun; others were sliding down the giant slide into the pool.

"Hey, you!" shouted the lifeguard. "You have to wear a bathing suit here."

"Oh!" said Leo. "I didn't know that."

Suddenly the lifeguard realized that Leo was a lion.

"Help!" he shouted. "A lion! A ferocious lion!" He started climbing up the giant slide. Leo climbed after him.

"Please wait!" he called to the lifeguard. "I just want to ask you something."

But the lifeguard slid down into the pool. Leo slid down after him. The lifeguard and everyone else in the pool started splashing Leo with water.

"I am only big on the outside. Inside I am small and huggable," Leo cried. "Would someone please give me a little hug!" But because Leo had swallowed so much water, he sounded as if he were roaring.

Leo climbed out of the pool and shook himself. Water flew in all directions.

"You'll see!" Leo said. "I'll find someone brave enough to pet a lion."

Leo headed for the zoo.

"Are you brave enough to pet a lion?" Leo asked the zoo keeper.

"Hhmm," mumbled the keeper, leafing through a thick book.

"Would *you* give me a little pat?" Leo asked.

"I'm busy," said the zookeeper, and continued leafing through the book.

"Please give me a little pat!" begged Leo.

"Oh, all right," said the zookeeper, and looked at the clock.

"Our zoo lions are about to get their daily pats. One lion more or less won't make a difference."

There was a knock on the door, and the lion keeper led in two lions.

"Now lie down next to those lions," said the zookeeper. "That way it will be easier to pet you."

"But I want to sit on your lap like Katrinka does."

"Absolutely not!" said the zookeeper.

So Leo got up and left. He didn't want to be "one lion more or less."

Leo was getting desperate. He had been wandering around all day trying to find someone who would not be afraid to pet him. Soon it would get dark. Soon Katrinka would be sitting on Mr. Brown's shoulder purring in his ear. Leo had to find someone who would pet him! He just had to!

It was then that he spied the engineer on the locomotive.

"Good evening," said Leo, jumping up on the moving engine.

"Would you please give me a little pat?"

"A lion!" shouted the engineer. "A ferocious lion!"

"Please don't be afraid of me," begged Leo. "I am a very tame lion."

But the engineer was horrified. He jumped off the locomotive. Leo was about to leap off after him when the train began to pick up speed.

The rushing wind brushed through Leo's mane and gently stroked his fur. Leo liked that. It was almost as good as being petted.

Soon it began to get dark. The train traveled on and on, farther and farther.

23

Leo was lulled to sleep.

A sudden jolt and a grinding noise awoke Leo the next morning. The train had stopped.

Leo rubbed his sleepy eyes and looked around.

Near the train stood two large birds, their heads buried in the sand.

And up ahead the tracks were covered by a mountain of sand. In fact there was sand everywhere.

Leo was in the desert. At the edge of the desert there were palm trees, and beyond, an oasis shimmered on the horizon.

It was hot. Very hot.

Leo guessed that he must be in Africa, or someplace that looked like Africa.

Happily he stretched himself out in the shade of the train.
In the evening, when it got cooler, a lioness came over to
the locomotive. Her name was Lea.

Leo had never seen anyone so beautiful. Her golden fur was like velvet.

Leo told Lea many exciting stories about his journey.
The only thing he didn't tell her was that he had been asleep for most of the trip.

Lea comes every night now.

Leo rarely thinks of Mr. Brown and Katrinka anymore.

He has fallen in love with Lea.

He strokes her golden fur gently with his huge paw, and Lea gently strokes his mane.

Sometimes Leo tells her, "You are very brave, Lea."

"Why so?" Lea asks.

"Because *you* are not afraid to pet a lion."

Then they both roll on the desert sands and laugh.

Leo the lion is not lonely anymore.

The shifting sands have long since covered up the locomotive. But that's all right—Leo has no intention of leaving. There are palm trees at the edge of the desert, and beyond, an oasis shimmers on the horizon.